HOME

Chapter 1: Escaping Homework

It was Monday, and Michael and Jeremy were stressing about the project they had to get done for school. Michael was a nice but shy 12-year-old, and Jeremy was a really outgoing and funny 10-year-old. They lived in Laguna Niguel, California. They had been goofing around all weekend and Monday, too, since it was a day off. They had forgotten that their project was due on Tuesday. In their bedroom, trying to sleep, Michael and Jeremy were really scared that their grades might go down.

"I don't want to go to school tomorrow," said Michael.

"Me neither," Jeremy agreed.

It was freezing outside, and they were very cozy under their warm blankets. But they would much rather freeze than have a deadline over their heads.

"Hey how about this, we escape right now and go to Europe?!" Michael said as a joke.

"Sure, why not?" said Jeremy.

"Wait I didn't–"

"Let's go, come on!"

So off they went. They took their parents' car.

On the way to LAX airport, Michael was driving and Jeremy was sitting in the passenger seat. Michael was surprisingly good at driving even though he hadn't even tried it before. Jeremy booked their tickets on his phone. They decided to go to France first.

"What do you want to do in France?" Jeremy asked.

"I want to go to some museums," Michael responded.

"Like the Louvre?" Jeremy asked.

"Good idea, what paintings do you want to see there?"

"I want to see the Mona Lisa, not online, but for real this time." Jeremy saw the Mona Lisa online during art class, he liked her mysterious expression, that's what made her famous.

"Okay!" Michael said.

"Is there anything you want to eat?" Jeremy asked.

"I want to eat real French onion soup – it's cheesy and delicious, I wonder how it is in France."

Ohio Air
Cleveland
Air Ohio
Columbus
Ohio Airlines
Cincinnati
Ohio airways
Kennel

About an hour later, Michael and Jeremy arrived at the airport. They didn't need to check any baggage, because all they brought was a fanny pack for each of them. After the security checkpoint, Michael and Jeremy were very thirsty. Michael had remembered to bring some cash in case they needed it, so they bought some snacks and drinks. Michael looked at the souvenirs– he wanted a fridge magnet. He picked one with pictures of the Los Angeles skyline.

"But we didn't bring the fridge!" said Jeremy.

"It's not for our fridge," Michael said. "We can give magnets as gifts to people who help us on the way."

"I'm so excited to get on the plane!" said Jeremy.

"Let's see what seats we have on the plane…WHAT?! You booked first class?!" Michael said with disbelief.

"Yep!"

"How did you get that much money?"

"Now, let's not worry about that, let's just enjoy ourselves!"

So Michael and Jeremy went to the first class lounge. They had great food there such as French onion soup, french fries, French vanilla yogurt, and chicken nuggets.

They ordered everything on the menu that had the word French in it!

The French Onion soup was pretty good, and Michael couldn't wait for more in France.

After about an hour in the lounge, it was time to go to the boarding gate.

Jeremy showed a staff member their passports that they stole from their parents' safe, and they boarded the plane, first class style.

The flight attendants handed them drinks.

Michael got orange juice, what he usually gets, but Jeremy decided to get champagne.

Chapter 2: Bon Voyage!

The seats in first class were amazing. They had lots of cushioning, they were very spacious, and they even had sliding doors around them. Michael and Jeremy played with them, sliding them open and closed!

"How much money did this cost, Jeremy?" asked Michael.

"I said, let's enjoy ourselves, remember?"

"Okay, fine, but just make sure it wasn't too expensive, or else mom and dad won't like it."

So Michael and Jeremy ordered meals. They ordered baguettes, macaroons, and their favorite French food, French onion soup. After they were done eating, Michael and Jeremy tried to sleep. The airplane's engines roared like a really strong gust of wind.

"I can't fall asleep," said Michael to Jeremy.

"Me neither," Jeremy replied, "but another cool thing about first class is that you get a lot of surprises!"

Jeremy pulled out a box made out of cloth, and inside there were noise-canceling headphones and an eye-mask. Both things were really helpful in terms of sleeping. So they slept until dawn, and when Michael woke up, he was fascinated when he saw the Eiffel Tower outside his window.

"Jeremy, Jeremy, wake up!" Michael said, throwing his slipper across the aisle to hit Jeremy. The slipper landed on Jeremy's leg, bunching up his blanket.

"What?" Jeremy said, sounding exhausted.

"Look, come to my seat and look out this window."

Jeremy rubbed his eyes, put on his slippers, and walked across the aisle to Michael's seat. Paris spread out below.

"Wow, that's a nice view! I'm so excited!".

"Yeah, so am I!" Michael agreed.

After about half an hour, Michael and Jeremy's plane landed in the Charles de Gaulle International Airport in Paris, France. They walked out of the plane, had a bathroom break, went through customs, and caught a taxi to go to their hotel.

In the taxi, Michael and Jeremy stared out of the window during the long car ride to the hotel. The Charles de Gaulle airport was far from the city center of Paris itself. There were lots of fields, flowers, and it was raining. Jeremy booked the hotel on his phone.

"I'm so bored!" said Jeremy.

"Don't say that, let's try to spot some animals outside!" said Michael.

"Okay!"

Michael and Jeremy were in shock as they saw lots of frogs, deer, and rabbits hopping around and grazing near a swamp. They also saw rabbits grazing in a field. A farmer was herding cows into a barn, and a deer was looking for moss on a rock.

"The animals are cool," said the taxi driver. "Bonjour and hello there, young Americans."

"Hello, what's your name?" Jeremy replied.

"Pierre, and you?"

"My name is Jeremy, and he's my brother Michael."

"Enchanté– Nice to meet you!"

Pierre turned on classical music, and they all enjoyed it. It was violin. They felt calm.

"Are you hungry? Would you like a surprise?" asked Pierre.

"Yes, please!" said Jeremy.

Pierre pulled over. He jumped out and went to the back of the car. He had a special mini fridge in the trunk. He came back with a paper box.

"I love snacks," Pierre told them, and handed them the box.

It was macaroons!

"Can I have most of them?" asked Jeremy.

"Take as many as you want," Pierre told them. Pierre took three. Michael took one. Jeremy took eight.

"So, where in the United States do you come from?" Pierre asked.

"California," Michael replied.

"Where are your parents?"

"Uh…we came here without them."

"I see, I'll tell you this, I did the same thing when I was your age. I went to Switzerland, I wanted to see the mountains."

"What did you do there?"

"I skied, I had cheese fondue, and I enjoyed the cold crisp air."

"Were your parents mad?" Michael asked.

Pierre laughed. "Oui! They were really mad! Eventually, they calmed down. They were relieved that I was home again. And I had so much fun in Switzerland."

Michael felt relieved that eventually Pierre's parents weren't angry. He finished his macaroon, it was delicious. He looked over at Jeremy.

"Jeremy, you have crumbs on your face."

"Where?"

"Your eyebrow!"

Jeremy laughed.

Pierre pulled up to the hotel. They paid Pierre in US Dollars. The ride was $150 USD, but they gave him $200. Pierre gave them his phone number so they could contact him. Michael gave him a magnet that said Los Angeles.

"Merci! My refrigerator can't wait to see California." Pierre called out the window, and drove away.

After Pierre dropped Michael and Jeremy off at the hotel, they were amazed at how tall it was. It was a metal skyscraper, next to the Eiffel Tower. They both wanted to go shopping and get a souvenir for their parents. They were so excited they decided to go shopping before checking in!

Their mom liked Dior clothing, and their dad liked simple black clothes. While they were shopping they decided to come back and shop more the next day, they just wanted to look around today. It started to get late.

There was a lot to see! They saw the Eiffel Tower lit up, and they saw the Paris skyline. There was graffiti that was colorful and interesting. The words were in French and they couldn't read them, they only knew a little French. There was a bakery that had baguettes half Jeremy's size. The neighborhood was peaceful. They wanted to go to the museum, but it was too late, so they went back to the hotel to check in. They were a little tired, and glad to be at the hotel.

There was a problem though— they forgot their passports in Pierre's car! They didn't want to bother Pierre because it was so late.

"I think we should call him tomorrow," said Jeremy.

"But if we want a hotel room, we have to have our passports," said Michael. He began to sweat. "What are we going to do now?"

"I don't know, maybe let's sleep in a field or something?" replied Jeremy.

"Like on the grass?"

"Yeah.. let's get it over with."

"I guess…WAIT! We can buy a tent and sleeping bags so we won't be cold tonight!"

"Great Idea! We can use the gear anytime so that we don't have to book hotels! Less work for me!" said Jeremy.

So Michael and Jeremy went to a 24 hour camping store, exchanged some USD to euros, and bought everything they needed that night.

They found an empty field with trees, and set their tent up by the light of their flashlights. Then they tucked their sleeping bags into the tent. It was cozy. It smelled of grass and wildflowers. There were small bushes of red roses. There was a rabbit that had a little white butt.

They wanted to make a campfire, but Michael was afraid the grass would catch fire and burn everything down. So, they were a little cold without a campfire, and they got tired setting up the tent. After tucking into the sleeping bags, Then, before they knew it, they were asleep.

PASSPORT

In the morning, they cleaned up their tents. They packed them up in their bags. The grass was wet with morning dew. It was a cloudy day.

"I'm afraid it's going to rain," said Michael.

"You're always worried about things," said Jeremy. They did not have raincoats.

"Let's get our passports from Pierre," said Michael.

"I want a French breakfast," said Jeremy.

"Let's get our passports first, that's more important," Michael said.

"Fine."

They called Pierre and he came. He was happy to see them.

"My macaroon-lovers!" said Pierre. He gave them their passports.

"Can I have another macaroon?" asked Jeremy.

"Sorry, I ran out," said Pierre.

"Aww, man." Said Jeremy.

"Thank you for our passports," Michael said.

"We are getting breakfast and going to the Louvre, do you want to come?" Jeremy asked.

"Sure!" said Pierre. They put all their tents and gear in the trunk, and drove off together.

They stopped at a cafe. Jeremy got his French breakfast, with a lot of macaroons.

"That's a lot of sugar for the morning," said a stranger sitting next to Jeremy.

"You speak English really well," said Jeremy. He had crumbs all over his plate, and he started licking them.

"Les Americains!" said the stranger, and left.

Someone at the cafe was playing piano. It was not a song they knew. Michael went up to the manager and said something.

"Is Michael getting more food?" asked Pierre.

"I don't know," said Jeremy, still licking the plate.

Even though he seemed shy, Michael went straight to the piano. The piano player got up and let Michael sit down. He played piano quickly. His fingers flew all over the place.

"He's gotten better," said Jeremy, chewing his last macaroon.

"Oh that's cool," said Pierre.

Michael played Chopin. People clapped when he finished.

Then they were off to the Louvre!

Chapter 4: Chasing the Mona Lisa

After a twenty minutes' drive, Michael, Jeremy, and Pierre arrived at the Louvre. Pierre drove the car into the underground garage, and they went up to the pyramid entrance of the Louvre. The pyramid was huge, and it went downstairs to the lobby. Since Michael, Jeremy, and Pierre didn't have tickets, they had to wait longer. After waiting for about ten minutes, they were let in.

"Let's go see the Mona Lisa!" Jeremy said.

"I think it's too crowded now, maybe we should see other paintings," said Pierre.

Jeremy agreed, and they went to see the Venus de Milo statue, the Winged Victory of Samothrace, and the Raft of the Medusa. Finally, after half an hour of exploring the huge museum, the crowd at the Mona Lisa lessened.

"Now it's the perfect time to see the Mona Lisa," said Michael.

So they went to the Mona Lisa. Michael, Jeremy, and Pierre were really fascinated because none of them had seen the Mona Lisa in person before.

"Let's take some photos. Your parents will be amazed when they see you at the Mona Lisa!" said Pierre.

"Great idea!" Michael and Jeremy said.

So all three posed in front of the Mona Lisa. On the third picture they snapped, though, they saw a man with a bushy beard in a mask who took the Mona Lisa!

"Oh mon Dieu! That guy just stole the Mona Lisa!" exclaimed Pierre, who was frantically searching for a security guard.

"We should catch him before he gets away!" said Michael.

"Quick!" Jeremy yelled.

The police began running after the guy who stole the Mona Lisa, and Pierre, Michael, and Jeremy followed them. Before long, the robber got into his car in the parking garage, and the police got into their car, too. Michael and Jeremy got into Pierre's car, and they all followed the robber's red Porsche. They got on the phone with the police officers, Louis and Gabriel, and got word that the police had hacked into the robber's GPS. The GPS said the robber was only a few minutes ahead of them. When the police saw the robber's destination, four words came out of the walkie-talkie:

"Il va à l'aéroport."

"He's going to the airport to escape," Pierre translated.
When they got to the airport and checked in, the police realized that the GPS said that the robber's location changed dramatically. His altitude changed drastically, too. That could only mean one thing: his plane must have taken off. So Michael, Jeremy, Pierre, and the police officers wanted to go after them.

"What should we do to try to get him?" said Michael.
"Let's just say I have a secret weapon," said Pierre.
"Whoa, cool! What is it?" asked Jeremy.
"Jeremy, it's supposed to be a secret!" said Michael.
"Oops," said Jeremy.

Chapter 5: Pierre's Secret

The Three were pretty hungry after using much of their brain energy, so they took a break at the rest stop. Jeremy wanted some macaroons because he knew Pierre restocked them. So he went back to the trunk and opened the fridge. He saw a button on the door, so he pressed it. Then, it started playing music.

"How do you open this thing?" said Jeremy, whose voice was muffled in the loud music.

"Jeremy, you do realize that there is a handle, right?" said Pierre.

"Oh yeah," realized Jeremy.

"My minifridge is actually a supercomputer, faster than anyone else's in the world," said Pierre.

"Wow!" said Michael.

"It is super, it dispenses macaroons!" said Jeremy while eating one.

"How did you get it?" asked Michael.

"I built it," said Pierre.

"Then why do you drive a cab?" asked Jeremy.

"Driving is my passion," answered Pierre, "It is far more interesting than you might think. I get to meet new people and learn about them, all in my little cab."

"Woah, that is really cool!" said Michael.

"Yeah," agreed Jeremy.

"I used to work for the government, but now, I work for my customers," said Pierre.

"Ooh, so you're an undercover FBI agent!" said Jeremy.

"Jeremy, the FBI is only in the United States. It's the CIA that's international," said Michael.

"But Pierre's French, so it's neither," said Jeremy.

"You don't understand," said Michael.

"My friends, nobody understands," said Pierre. "Jeremy, do you need more macaroons?"

"Ehh, I'm good," said Jeremy quietly.

They got back onto the freeway toward the airport. Jeremy was feeling car sick from eating too many macaroons, so he pulled down the windows. It smelled of gasoline and dirty snow. It was freezing outside, so Jeremy quickly shut the window.

"Do you miss your old job?" asked Michael.

"Well, I love whatever life gives me," said Pierre.

"It would be cool if we could find the Mona Lisa ourselves," said Jeremy.

Michael and Pierre agreed, and they decided on pursuing their own investigation with Pierre's secret weapon. They could also hack into the police officers' GPS, too.

<u>Chapter 6: To Venice!</u>

They drove fast and arrived quickly at Charles DeGaulle Airport. They waited for an hour, then boarded the plane to Venice. Venice is a city in northeastern Italy, it is an island with many canals, which are its "roads". They saw many gondola boats being rowed by tightly costumed men in stripes and high-waisted pants. Some carried passengers, while others carried food and cargo. Some boats were wooden and had roofs, some were metal, some had motors. The water was a murky dark greenish blue. They saw the Rialto Bridge, an iconic bridge that is seen on most Venice postcards, defined by straight lines and curves above a giant arch over the river. "The air smells like fish," said Jeremy, sniffing the air.

"Yeah, it's probably the water that smells like fish," replied Michael.

"I like the smell of fish!" said Pierre.

The Three quickly realized that they had no time to waste. Pierre took out the GPS and it said that Rob was at a ferry station. When Pierre zoomed in closer, he realized that those ferries were heading toward the JW Marriott hotel. The hotel is on a separate island that is pretty far from downtown Venice.

Michael, Jeremy, and Pierre ran down the dark alleyways lined with shops and historic buildings untouched by time. The alleyways smelled from the sewage that ran through the underground, but the Three didn't complain. They ran and ran. They were starting to have other concerns.

"I'm hungry!" said Jeremy, out of nowhere, panting from the distance they'd run.

"How can you be hungry when it smells like this?" asked Michael, losing more of his breath with every word.

"Here," said Pierre to Jeremy, stopping finally, "take this."He tossed an extra macaron from his pocket and leaned forward on his knees to catch his breath.

Jeremy ate the macaron sitting on a stair, and Michael and Pierre also sat to look at the GPS and see where Rob had gone. They needed a break badly, considering how far they had run. Sure enough, Rob's location on the GPS was in the middle of the sea. That meant he was already on the ferry, which wouldn't be back for another forty minutes. The Three realized how far they still were from the JW Marriott ferry station, but Pierre discovered that there was a ferry about to leave not far from them. So Michael, Jeremy, and Pierre ran as fast as they could to the ferry. Michael paid the 5 euros for each of them, and they boarded the boat.

"It will take fifteen minutes for this ferry to take us to our stop," said Pierre.

"That's okay, since I was dreading having forty minutes doing absolutely nothing," said Jeremy.

They all laughed, and before they knew it, they were at the ferry station to JW Marriott. The station smelled like fish, but The Three were all used to it now. Twenty minutes later, the ferry arrived at the hotel. On the ferry, Pierre, Michael, and Jeremy discussed what they were going to do next. But first, they needed to check where Rob was. Pierre took the GPS out of his bag, and they saw that Rob was at the lobby of the hotel. The GPS updated, and Rob was now on the tenth floor of the building.

After closely watching the GPS, The Three discussed a game plan of what they should do. Since the GPS was not exact enough, there was no possibility that they would find Rob's room. So they agreed to get a room, rest for the night, and work on catching Rob the next day. When Michael, Jeremy, and Pierre got to the hotel, they did just that. Pierre did the booking, and they found themselves in a pretty large room on the fourth floor. So, after ordering room service for dinner (with French onion soup, of course), they all went to bed.

Jeremy woke up at 5:30 AM because he couldn't sleep any more. At first, he was about to turn on the TV, but then he realized that he should check the GPS, just in case. Jeremy pressed the on button, and rubbed his eyes for better vision. The GPS said that Rob was on the ground floor. Jeremy guessed he was getting breakfast.

"Michael! Pierre! Wake up!" yelled Jeremy.

"Whaaaa..?" said Michael with a tired expression.

"Rob is getting breakfast, so we better hurry up!" exclaimed Jeremy.

"I have to brush my teeth first," said Michael. "C'mon Jeremy, brush your teeth before we go."

"Do I have to?" said Jeremy.

"Yeah, of course, unless you want to look like an ogre," replied Michael. Pierre instantly woke up, got dressed, and brushed his teeth without saying anything. They checked the GPS one more time just to make sure Rob was still there, packed their belongings, and left the room.

On the way downstairs in the elevator, Michael, Jeremy, and Pierre planned to corner Rob on his way out of the hotel. They walked to the hotel restaurant for breakfast, told a staff member their room number, and instantly spotted Rob enjoying his croissant.

His suitcase and a rectangular package wrapped in cloth, about 3' by 2', was next to him. It must be the Mona Lisa! He was probably planning to leave after breakfast. Rob spotted Jeremy, and he knew he was in trouble. So Rob stuffed the croissant in his pocket to save for later, grabbed his package and the suitcase, and dashed out the hotel door.

"Quick! We need to catch him!" said Jeremy.

"I need to check out first," said Pierre.

"Okay, but do it quickly– we don't have much time!" yelled Jeremy.

So Pierre checked out quickly, and they went to the ferry station where they expected Rob to be. He wasn't there. All Michael, Jeremy, and Pierre could see in the distance was the ferry toward downtown Venice. And when they checked their GPS, they knew Rob was in that ferry.

"Ugh… he got away again!" complained Jeremy.

"It's okay, we'll catch him eventually," said Michael.

The sky was foggy, and it looked like it was going to rain soon in Venice. The Three sat on a bench waiting for the next ferry to come. When it did come, Michael and Jeremy were almost asleep, and Pierre had to drag them on the ferry.

The ferry had a roof with an inside and outside area. They went outside. Nobody felt talkative until Pierre took out his fishing rod. They caught lots of fish and let the fish back into the sea, and that was fun. Before they knew it, they were at the hotel ferry station in downtown Venice.

Sitting on a stair, Michael, Jeremy, and Pierre all checked the GPS. Rob was again heading for the airport, so they had to get another boat, this time to the airport. When they got off the boat, Pierre checked the GPS. He saw that Rob was again on a plane. This time, towards Athens. Jeremy instantly got out his phone and booked the airplane tickets to Athens.

So Michael, Jeremy, and Pierre were about to go check in. Michael and Jeremy found seats in the waiting area, and sat down. Pierre showed the staff member their tickets. When Pierre got back, he was shaking his head with a worried expression.

"What happened?" asked Jeremy, who was very confused.

"I know this sounds ridiculous, but our flight is scheduled for next week," said Pierre.

"What?! I thought I booked them for today at 3 PM," said Jeremy.

"You should have checked more carefully," said Michael, who was worried, too, "Let me see the tickets…Are you serious? You booked them next week... for 3 AM!"

"Oopsies, sorry guys."

"Are there any other flights today?" asked Michael.

"All the flights to Athens are full," said Pierre.

"What are we going to do, then?" asked Michael.

"Maybe we just sneak into the cargo hold!" said Jeremy.

So The Three went out the emergency door, which surprisingly didn't have an alarm. Then, as one Aegean Airlines flight was about to close its cargo hold doors, Michael, Jeremy, and Pierre jumped in in the nick of time. Then, they took off.

In the dark cargo hold, Pierre took out his flashlight from his bag. The engine rumbled. Then, he rummaged in his bag and found the GPS, stored safely inside the front pocket.

"Where is Rob now?" asked Jeremy.

"Uhh… the GPS says that he is hovering over Ioannina, which is a city in northern Greece," said Pierre.

"I think he will go to the hotel and rest for the day," Michael said, "Until then, we'll have to wait the two hours left of his flight."

So Michael, Jeremy, and Pierre sat next to the flashlight and tracked Rob's location. Half an hour later, Rob had landed in Athens. Another half hour passed, and Rob was leaving the airport and going toward a Hilton hotel. After their plane landed, Michael, Jeremy, and Pierre dashed out of the cargo hold as the maintenance crew outside were shooting confused looks at them. Since his legs fell asleep in the airplane from sitting so long, Michael tripped and fell onto the ground outside of the airplane. Embarrassed, Michael got up and started running. They jumped a fence, and they were now outside airport territory.

"We should get a taxi now so we can get to the hotel Rob is at," said Pierre.

"Good idea," said Jeremy, "Michael, take out your euros to be ready."

"I think I ran out of money, so I will go to an ATM to get some euros."

"Okay, no rush," Pierre said while checking the GPS, "it looks like Rob is resting at the hotel for the night."

So Michael got 200 euros from the ATM, and apparently the hotel shuttle was free, so they took that. When they got to the hotel, they realized that 200 euros was not enough for a room. So they took out their camping gear they bought back in Paris, and set it up in a field. After eating dinner in the hotel restaurant, they went outside and fell asleep.

Chapter 9: Good Morning Greece

The next day, Jeremy woke up at around seven in the morning and knew what he had to do. He was really groggy and tired, so much so that his arms felt like noodles. He got the GPS from Pierre's bag and searched for where Rob was. He was surprised to see that Rob was still in his room because Rob usually was an early riser. Jeremy foolishly thought that since he was still in his room, they could sleep more. This, however, they would regret in the near future. When Jeremy woke up a second time, Michael and Pierre were still waking up. He checked Pierre's phone and was shocked to see that it was 10 in the morning. Pierre reached into his backpack and got out his GPS.

"Quick, guys! Rob is somewhere else! He left the hotel!" said Pierre.

"Yeah, Jeremy get up!" said Michael.

Jeremy got up and put on his clothes. The Three packed up their gear and went to hunt Rob down. Michael used the rest of his euros on a taxi to Rob's location. Rob had gone to the Parthenon, which is a really famous landmark in Greece. It was a monument built by the Athenians to worship Athena, the Greek goddess of wisdom and warfare. It was made of gray stone. It had a roof with pillars, parts of the Parthenon were damaged because of wars, earthquakes, and invasions.

When The Three arrived, they saw Rob with a camera taking a picture with a statue. Then, when nobody was looking, Rob stole the statue's shoulder! Immediately, an alarm went off and the police started chasing after Rob. Unfortunately, Rob was too fast and got to his car before the police did, and sped off. Pierre took out the GPS and tracked Rob's location. Rob was in his rental car and was heading toward the dock, where ferries left for the Greek islands.

When Michael, Jeremy, and Pierre arrived at the dock, Rob was again in the middle of the sea, according to the GPS. That meant he was already on the ferry. Michael and Pierre tracked the GPS closely and were researching where the ferries went while Jeremy booked the ferry tickets. He was careful to check the date and time this time.

"We found out where Rob is going," said Michael.

"Oui, indeed!" said Pierre.

"He is on track to go to Santorini."

"Where is that?" said Jeremy.

"You know the place where there are white buildings with blue domes?" said Michael.

"Yeah," said Jeremy.

"That's where he is going."

"He must plan on having a fancy dinner with the Mona Lisa!"

They all laughed while walking toward the ferry. It would be a long ride, approximately seven hours. They were looking forward to a nice, long break. On the ferry, they had a big lunch of pasta, fried rice, and, of course, French onion soup, since they didn't eat breakfast.

Chapter 10: To Santorini!

After resting for a bit, Pierre checked the GPS.

"Hey, Rob arrived at Santorini!" said Pierre.

"Too bad we still have three hours left on this ride," said Jeremy.

"But at least we guessed where he went," said Michael, "that's something."

They checked the GPS again, and Rob was near a hotel called Canaves Oia, in a town called (you guessed it) Oia. His location paused, so they assumed that he was stopping there for the night. After around three hours, Michael, Jeremy, and Pierre finally got off the boat. When they stepped out of the door, the heat hit them hard. Before long, all three of them were sweating. Rob seemed like he was relaxing in his room while Michael, Jeremy, and Pierre got onto the hotel shuttle. Surprisingly, Santorini was basically a desert. The roads were dusty with the sun beating down on the buildings. Since The Three still didn't have any money, they had to camp outside again. They set up their tents and hammocks and rested there for a while. That was until Michael spotted Rob's location had moved again. He was at a really famous sunset place, also known as the town of Thira, probably having the time of his life.

"We should go there not only to find Rob, but to enjoy the sunset there!" said Pierre.

"Yeah, let's not miss out on the fun!" said Jeremy.

"I agree!" said Michael.

So Pierre called a taxi and paid, since Michael and Jeremy didn't have any euros left. They got to Thira, checked the GPS, and realized that Rob had gone back to the hotel. Michael, Jeremy, and Pierre didn't care. Having fun was more important to them in that moment!

They were on a steep hill. A small ocean breeze ruffled their hair. It was humid. They gazed at the sunset, practically daydreaming. The orange and the yellow mixed with the pale blue to create an explosion of colors. Michael, Jeremy, and Pierre took tons of photos. They walked down the hill, bought some souvenirs, and had a nice dinner at a seafood restaurant. Then, they went back to their tents and hammocks and slept well.

Meanwhile, Rob had different plans. In his hotel room, he packed up the wrapped Mona Lisa into his suitcase. Rob had booked a flight for Shanghai a day earlier, but he had to go to Rome first to see his business partner, Benito, who abducted the Starry Night. There, they discussed what to do with all of their riches that they would earn. For now, though, there was still escaping to do.

"We have been tricked!" announced Pierre, right after they woke up. Rob was in Rome now, and his location was moving toward the airport.

"What are we going to do now?" said Jeremy.

"I say we predict where Rob goes next. Let's wait for him to get onto the plane and then we can search for his flight," said Michael.

"That's actually smart!" said Jeremy.

"Thanks, remember to brush your teeth." Said Michael.

So they ate breakfast at the hotel restaurant, packed up their camping gear, and took a taxi to the airport. There, they waited for Rob's location to move. After around three hours of waiting, Rob's location finally began to shift. Michael and Pierre immediately researched the flights departing from Rome and found out that he was going all the way to Shanghai, China.

They needed money. They had used all of their euros on expensive things that were not going to benefit them later on.

"If we get money later on, let's be more careful on what we spend it on," said Pierre.

"If we get any," said Michael.

The Three sat next to the windows in the airport. Looking out to the blue sea, they were upset that they didn't have enough money to book the flight. Suddenly, a man walked by and noticed that they were gloomy.

"You guys look tired, what's going on?" asked the man.

"Who are you?" asked Jeremy.

"I'm Pablo, I came from Spain."

"Nice to meet you," said Michael.

"So, what's going on?" asked Pablo.

Pierre looked him over and said, "I think I can trust you because you look honest. We're trying to chase down a robber who stole the Mona Lisa, except he is too fast."

"Oh wow, I don't want the Mona Lisa to be stolen, do you guys need any help?" said Pablo, surprised.

"Yeah, we're short on money, that's been a big issue," said Jeremy, "This is why we are sitting here."

"Hey guys, wanna know a cool story?" said Pablo.

"Okay!" said Jeremy.

"So I was just minding my own business gambling at my local casino and then I won 100,000 euros!" said Pablo, who was very excited.

"Oh wow, that's nice. Is that why you're on vacation?" asked Michael.

"Yep," said Pablo, "Want 20,000?"

"Is this real?" said Pierre.

"Yeah, but the only catch is that you guys have to give some away," said Pablo.

"Sure, we'll do that!" said The Three.

So they thanked Pablo and exchanged phone numbers. As Pablo was walking out of the airport, Michael shouted, "Make sure you go to the seafood restaurant that I sent you, and see the sunset at Thira!"

"I sure will!" shouted Pablo.

Jeremy booked the tickets with Pablo's money.

"Guys, for your information, we're going to Turkey!" said Jeremy.

"What? I thought we were going to China!" said Pierre.

"It's just a transfer. Then we will go to China!" said Jeremy.

"Sounds like a plan!" said Michael and Pierre.

So they checked into the airport, went through security, and waited for their flight. While they were waiting, they decided to get some Turkish kebabs since they were going to Turkey. Michael and Pierre both got pork kebabs, while Jeremy got a Turkish wrap and some ice cream for dessert. After an hour or so, they boarded their flight. On the plane, they checked their GPS and saw that Rob was halfway to China. That meant he would have a six-hour head start over them. Even worse, he could be transferring to another place.

Luckily, however, when Rob landed, it seemed that he was going towards a hotel called Conrad. While he was going towards Conrad, Michael, Jeremy, and Pierre landed in Istanbul airport. So with that worry off their minds, The Three boarded the plane at Istanbul. They had a nice dinner on the plane, and slept. After four hours, they landed in Shanghai. Michael, Jeremy, and Pierre were jet lagged. However, that didn't stop them from checking Rob's location once again. As expected, Rob was in his hotel room. So, after getting through customs, Pierre used the money that Pablo gave them and exchanged it into Chinese yuan. Then, they took a taxi to the hotel Conrad.

"I want to sleep..." complained Michael.

"Yeah, me too, but we're almost there," said Jeremy.
After twenty minutes, they were there.

"Thanks for getting us here!" said Pierre as he handed the driver 1,000 yuan, which is about 150 dollars.

"Wow, thank you and you're welcome!" said the driver in English with a Mandarin accent. So, The Three checked in, went upstairs, and fell asleep.

The next day, Michael, Jeremy, and Pierre went through their normal routine of checking Rob's location. They woke up at around 10 AM because of jet lag, so that was pretty late. The GPS showed that Rob was in downtown Shanghai, near the Oriental Pearl Tower.

"Guys, quick! We need to see what Rob is up to!" said Jeremy.

"Okay, but let's eat breakfast first," said Michael.

"I agree." Said Pierre. "By the way, I have more macaroons. Who wants some?"

"Can I have all of them?" said Jeremy.

Michael stared at him. Jeremy gave him one.

"Thanks," said Michael. Jeremy ate the rest.

So they ate yogurt and macaroons for breakfast, and they took a bus to the tower. When Michael, Jeremy, and Pierre got there, Rob was just coming out of the main entrance. He was carrying a Mona Lisa-shaped rectangle covered in tin-foil.

"Go! Get him!" shouted Jeremy.

The Three ran after Rob, but he pulled out a grenade and aimed for them. Michael narrowly dodged the grenade as it hit the concrete sidewalk. It burst into flames, and rocks flew out from the pavement. Lots of people started screaming. Michael, Jeremy and Pierre stopped to make sure everyone near the grenade was okay. In that time, however, Rob the robber got away.

A little girl had been scratched, and Pierre offered to take her to the hospital to get bandaged. Her mom agreed. Michael and Jeremy followed Pierre, the little girl, and her mom to the hospital. The doctor said that the scratch was not that bad, and put some ointment on the little girl's leg. He gave the container of ointment to the mom and sent them on their way.

"I'll pay for the visit and the ointment," said Pierre on their way out.

"No, no, it's okay," said the little girl's mom.

"I will pay because we caused the robber to throw the grenade," said Pierre.

"Really? It's not your fault, it's his fault. It's very kind of you!"

"No problem, and by the way, my name is Pierre."

"My name is Mrs. Wang, but you can call me Zhu, my daughter's name is Mei."

So after that was taken care of, Zhu and Mei said goodbye and went on their way.

Michael, Jeremy, and Pierre checked their GPS and saw that Rob was at the hotel Conrad. They didn't feel like going back to the hotel, they were really hungry. Zhu had said that they couldn't leave Shanghai without going to Golden Basket Dim Sum, a really good restaurant. So they decided to go there. Instead of taking a taxi, they decided to take the bus instead, since it only cost 1 yuan per person.

Looking out the window, Michael, Jeremy, and Pierre saw the tall skyscrapers rising up against the blue sky. The ride to Golden Basket took around twenty minutes, which is a really good deal for just 1 yuan per person.

Chapter 13: From Disaster to Dumplings

When they walked into Golden Basket, a powerful aroma of fresh seafood and dim sum hypnotized them and led them to a table. They ordered the seafood dim sum, xiao long bao (XLB) soup dumplings, and the restaurant's famous specialty dumplings.

When they walked in, they were amazed by the architecture of the restaurant, and the smells, of course. Each table was encapsulated by a pagoda to make the experience more authentic. The carpet was dark red with a gold border. On their table, there was a sign that said "enjoy your food!" in Mandarin.

"This place is wonderful!" said Jeremy.

"I agree," said Michael, looking out of the wooden frame, "and Jeremy, don't put a dumpling on your head!"

"Who would do that to a dumpling so good? Now it's inedible!" said Pierre. Jeremy put it into his mouth anyway.

In the background, people were talking a lot while Michael, Jeremy, and Pierre were chewing loudly.

"Wow, this is so good!" said Michael.

"I agree," said Jeremy, with his mouth full.

"No wonder Zhu said that we couldn't leave without trying these!" said Pierre.

"And also, how's your hair-flavored dumpling?" Michael asked Jeremy.

"It's the best dumpling I've ever tasted!" answered Jeremy, still chewing.

When the bill came, they were surprised that the whole meal only cost 30 yuan, or a little more than 4 dollars.

After their delicious lunch at Golden Basket, The Three vowed to return to the restaurant. Then, they took the bus again, and headed back to the hotel. Pierre took a nap while Michael and Jeremy went to the store to buy some apple juice. Then, they read the books they had brought.

Pierre and Jeremy were reading comic books, Michael was reading historical fiction. Pierre's book was in French. Michael and Jeremy's books were in English. While reading, Pierre checked the GPS to make sure Rob hadn't gotten away. Then, they ordered takeout from Golden Basket for dinner since they liked the food so much. After eating, they slept.

Jeremy woke up first the next morning, as usual. He expected Rob to be at the airport because it was a very "Rob" thing to do. Sure enough, he was. So they went through their normal routine of going after Rob. They had dim sum for breakfast and went on their way. The Three checked the GPS, as usual. Rob was still in the airport, so the first thing they did was take a taxi. Surprisingly, the driver was the same driver that took them from the airport to the hotel.

The taxi driver was named Chen, and he was an older man. He was partly balding with a little gray hair, facial stubble, and big eyebrows. He looked and sounded very wise, with a kind smile. Chen wore simple clothing, a shirt with a coat, and some warm pants.

"Wow, Chen, the city you live in is so beautiful!" said Michael as he saw all the gorgeous buildings lining the Yangtze River. Traditional buildings designed to look like pagodas stood alongside modern skyscrapers shooting up into the sky.

"I agree!" said Jeremy.

"Next time you come here, I will take you to a nice dinner along the Yangtze River!" said Chen.

"Then we are coming back as soon as possible," said Pierre.

When they got to the airport, they tipped Chen 20,000 yuan, which is around 2,800 dollars. Chen was very surprised since that was a very unusual thing to do. He thanked them, gave them his number, and drove off.

Meanwhile, Rob was on his plane, about to take off. He made a call on his cell phone. Rob had gone to an international school and knew multiple languages. He used to be an interpreter, but later found out that stealing things was much more profitable. He talked with his business partner, Benito, in Italian, about what to do next. Benito had taken Starry Night from a New York museum and outrun the Italian police. He was hiding with the painting in Dubai. Benito and Rob planned to sell their paintings in Sapporo, Japan, to a greedy billionaire.

Rob didn't tell Benito about the incident with Michael, Jeremy, and Pierre because he didn't want to be embarrassed. Rob would meet Benito in Sapporo, and discuss where to sell their paintings.

Michael, Jeremy, and Pierre were on the plane enjoying a nice Japanese lunch. There was sushi, fish, rice, miso soup, and much more. Rob was landing in Sapporo. The Three decided to sleep for the three and a half hour flight. When they woke up, Rob was heading towards a hotel very far away from the city. So the first thing Michael, Jeremy, and Pierre did after getting through customs was get a shuttle to the hotel. They slept again, and when they got to the hotel, they checked the GPS and realized-- they were nowhere near Rob! While they were asleep, Rob had gotten off his shuttle and gone back to the city. He knew that Michael, Jeremy, and Pierre were on his tail.

"Rob tricked us again! He is back in the city." said Jeremy.

"This can't be good. He could be going back to the airport anytime now," said Michael.

"The best we can do now is follow him," said Pierre.

So they took the shuttle back to Sapporo airport. Rob was nearby at some person's house. So Michael went to the store and bought some camouflage ghillie suits as a disguise. The Three looked like old bushes. They were planning to surprise Benito and Rob when they least expected it. They went to the address where the GPS showed Rob. As bushes, The Three creeped around the house and blended in with the billionaire's landscaping.

Benito was with Rob, talking with the person who owned the house. Michael, Jeremy, and Pierrre listened closely to Rob, Benito, and the billionaire's conversation.

"700 million?" said one of the voices.

"750," said another.

"We have a deal!" said the first voice.

Then, as they were done negotiating, Michael, Jeremy, and Pierre started to chase after Benito and Rob.

Rob and Benito sprinted out of the yard, each with a plastic-wrapped painting in their arms, and The Three followed after them. Rob had the Mona Lisa and Benito had Starry Night. Rob reached into his pocket, hoping for a bomb, but then realized that he used his last bomb in China.

So Michael, Jeremy, and Pierre chased Rob and Benito alongside the beautiful mountains and cherry blossom trees. They chased them all the way to the train station, where they got in the same train car.

"Get them!" said Jeremy.

Michael and Jeremy went after Rob and the Mona Lisa first. But Rob tossed the plastic-wrapped Mona Lisa over their heads to Benito. Pierre went after him. But when they cornered Benito, he threw the paintings over to Rob. It went like this for some time, almost as if they were playing "monkey in the middle."

"We can't! They're too fast!" said Michael.

All this racket caused a police officer to come and separate them. Rob and Benito got away.

Chapter 15: Baking Up New Plans

So Michael, Jeremy and Pierre went to the airport to chase after Benito and Rob. The Three were very disappointed to have lost the paintings, so they went to a bakery and noodle shop for dinner. Michael ordered ramen, Pierre ordered mochi and Japanese croissants, and Jeremy ordered a chicken sandwich.

There, the baker noticed that Michael, Jeremy, and Pierre were looking depressed. So he invited them into his office to have a talk. The baker introduced himself as Kai, and listened to their situation. After that, he said that he would be happy to help them chase down Rob, anywhere in the world.

"But won't your boss get mad that you will be gone?" asked Michael.

"Oh, don't worry, because I am the boss," said Kai.

"That's good to hear!" said Pierre.

Jeremy was still munching on his chicken sandwich.

"The Mona Lisa is very important to me," Kai said. "Let me tell you a story...Once, when I was about your age, I went to the Louvre with my parents and siblings, and we saw the Mona Lisa. It was--" Kai seemed to be looking for the words.

"Mysterious?" Asked Jeremy.

"Beautiful?" Asked Michael.

"Everything." Answered Kai. "When we saw it we were both relaxed and energized."

"Yeah, guys, we need to rescue the Mona Lisa," said Jeremy. The Three checked the GPS.

"They are going to Los Angeles!" said Jeremy.

"Hey! That's near home!" said Michael.

"Yeah, I'm excited because I've always wanted to go there!" said Pierre. "I've heard fascinating stories from my friends. I want to see the landmarks of Los Angeles— the Hollywood sign and the stars on the Walk of Fame. And I want to try tacos for the first time!"

"Are there no taco places in France??" Asked Jeremy.

"Not many, and Los Angeles used to be Mexico. Mexico used to own the area around California and Texas, there is a lot of Mexican heritage. Your tacos are très authentic."

"That's cool to know," said Michael, interested to learn more.

"We need to get going," said Jeremy.

"I'm coming too," said Kai.

So The Four booked a flight, and waited while trying to spot Benito and Rob. But the GPS said Benito and Rob were on the other side of the terminal, getting a different flight. Michael, Jeremy, Pierre and Kai didn't bother chasing them since their own flight was boarding soon. After fifteen minutes, Michael, Jeremy, Pierre, and Kai were on the plane.

"How will we catch Rob and Benito in Los Angeles?" asked Jeremy.

"It is a big city, for sure," said Michael.

So The Three started discussing a game plan of how they could catch the greedy robbers. Kai listened. The robbers were all over the news now, and Michael, Jeremy, and Pierre were, too.

<u>Chapter 16: To Los Angeles!</u>

On the plane, they slept. After around ten hours, they arrived in Los Angeles. The Four got their bags from the overhead compartments and sprinted out of the airplane as fast as they could. Rob and Benito were already outside of the airport.

"How are they not tired from all this running?" said Michael.

"I don't know, ask them," said Pierre.

Jeremy was half asleep on a bench when Michael, Pierre and Kai called him to follow them into a taxi.

They didn't make it to the taxi. Someone came running up to them. It was Zhu! She was smiling.

"Zhu, what are you doing here?" asked Pierre, he was stunned.

"Hey, was the whole Japan thing a dream?" asked Jeremy.

"Hey I'm right here, it wasn't a dream!" said Kai.

"Maybe the plane took us back to China," said Michael.

"We are all in Los Angeles." Said Zhu. "Welcome to America! I came from China after seeing you on the news, I wanted to help...And I found you a special taxi."

They all went past the taxi stand.

A black car was there, waiting for them. Chen and Mei waved.

"We thought you guys might need backup to defeat the robbers," said Chen.

"And take them down once and for all!" said Zhu.

"Yeah!" said Mei.

So they drove off in Chen's rental car and went to track down Rob and Benito.

Benito and Rob were in a taxi now, heading towards Beverly Hills. They had to wear masks because their faces were well-known now. But that didn't stop them from going to the billionaire's house to sell their paintings. Little did they know, something was waiting for them there…

"Drive faster!" said Kai.

"I'm trying," said Chen, "I literally rented this car half an hour ago!"

They got out of the car in Beverly Hills, where Rob and Benito were supposed to be. There they were! Rob and Benito were talking on the street outside the billionaire's house. The Three— now Three Plus Four —were closely on Benito and Rob's tail. They chased after them. The robbers were sure that their enemies were gaining on them.

"Sono proprio dietro di noi!" said Rob. (They're right behind us!)

"Che cosa?! Cosa avrei potuto fare?" said Benito. (What?! What could I have done?)

Benito and Rob were panicking because they didn't have anything to distract the Three Plus Four. So their only choice was to hold off The Three Plus Four by force. Rob was trained in boxing, and Benito in karate. So they thought they could hold them off.

"Get them!" said Jeremy, for the millionth time. This time, however, the robbers were outnumbered greatly. But the robbers were experienced in fighting. So they rammed into Michael and Mei with their paintings. Michael and Mei fell to the ground. Benito and Rob used the same tactic with the rest of The Seven. But when they rammed into Kai, it was no use. Kai was a retired sumo wrestler, he wasn't going anywhere. Kai scared them off, and they had to run again.

So Benito and Rob ran off with their paintings. They fled to the Los Angeles home of the Japanese billionaire. The Seven dusted themselves off and chased after Benito and Rob. They cornered them in the Beverly Hills mansion. Even worse, the billionaire was not home yet, so Benito and Rob were locked out.

"Maybe we should get a locksmith," said Rob as he ran.

"Maybe we should get help! How did those guys get here?" said Benito.

Benito and Rob were running around in the front yard, but they couldn't escape. So the police came, and Rob and Benito went to jail.

It was time to return the paintings to their rightful owners. Jeremy had the idea to put the paintings on eBay and ask the museums to bid on them.

"It'll be fun!" said Jeremy. "We can send the money back once they've bid."

Pierre decided to hold on to the paintings and when he went back to France he would return them. But first he needed a taco.

Chapter 17: To The End!

"Actually, there's something even more important than a taco," said Pierre. "I think you boys should see your parents."

All of The Seven were feeling tired. It was time for Michael and Jeremy to go home. They brought everyone with them.

Michael and Jeremy's parents had been waiting for nearly a month for them to come back home. They were at home watching the news in pajamas when the doorbell rang.

They saw seven figures through the window, and they ran out.

"Oh my God!" said Michael and Jeremy's mom.

"We love you Pierre!" said both Michael's parents, and ran to hug him. Michael stood there and looked at Jeremy.

"What about us? Weren't you worried? How do you even know Pierre?" Asked Michael.

"Pierre contacted us every day." Said Michael's mom.

"When you left your passports in his car he called us, and we became friends," explained Michael's dad. "We didn't worry about you or Jeremy, we knew you were in good hands."

"We've been watching the news about you!" said Michael's mom.

Then Michael and Jeremy's parents hugged their sons so tightly they all fell on the ground. While there, Jeremy reached into his bag and took out something.

"Here's your wallet back," said Jeremy, handing it over to his dad. "I maxed out two credit cards."

"We got your teacher to give you an extension," said Michael's dad, with a smile. "Now your project is due tomorrow."

LAX